Home to **WYOMING**

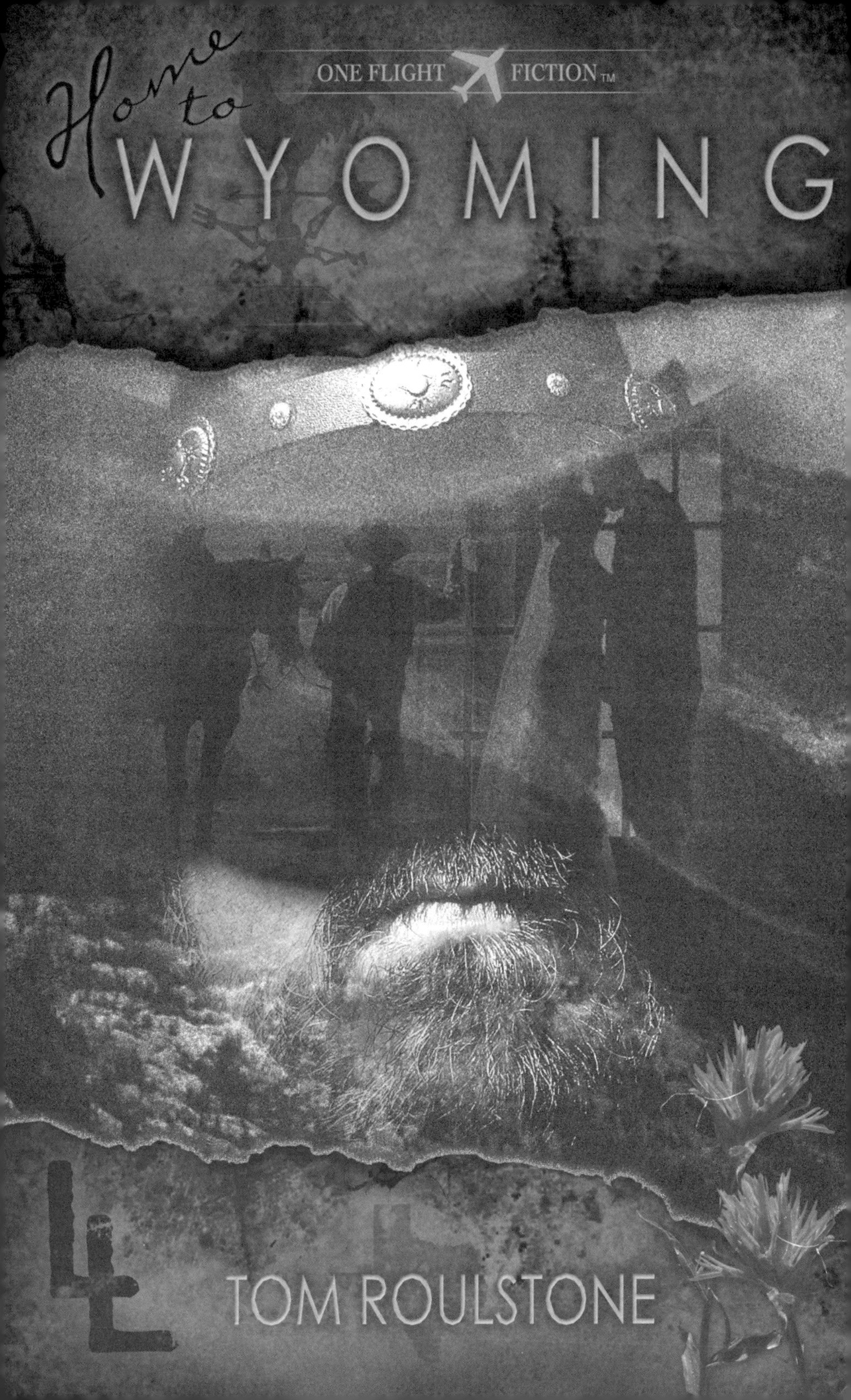
ONE FLIGHT FICTION™
Home to
WYOMING
TOM ROULSTONE

Edited by Christy Parr

Printed in the United States of America
First Printing: September 2006

Library of Congress Control Number: 2005939223

ISBN-13:   978-0-9773175-1-6
ISBN-10:   0-9773175-1-X

1

Jim Lattimore sat easy in the saddle as he surveyed the Double "L" ranch house and out buildings from the far side of the Little Laramie River. His eyes swept across the broad Laramie Valley and climbed to the tops of the distant mountains, now etched into a cerulean sky. Spring had turned the valley green and the sights, sounds and smells of new growth filled him with pleasure tinged with nostalgia. He recalled the happy days before his mother passed away, before he had run off to the dusty plains of west Texas fourteen years earlier. This ranch he loved would never be his, but it would always be home.

His eyes were drawn skyward as a vee of Canada geese silently glided north. Returning his gaze to the ranch buildings, he wondered at the lack of activity, although a wisp of smoke curling from the chimney witnessed that someone was home. The corral held only one horse.

He was about to ford the river when a rifle crack shattered the silence and a bullet buried itself in a tree trunk four feet from his head. Instinctively, he wheeled his horse Toby into the trees. Taking a huge gulp of air, he urged Toby upriver, screened by the trees bordering the river. Crossing at a second ford, he made a wide circle and approached the ranch house from the rear. Tethering his horse in the trees, he removed his spurs, looped them over the saddle horn and continued on foot. Easing around the corner of the house, he spied his quarry crouching behind a wagon. Dressed in baggy clothes with two auburn pigtails hanging down from under a battered straw hat, the shooter stared across the river.

Coming up from behind, Jim leaned over and snatched the Winchester away. The girl cried out as she turned to face him. "Give me back my gun," she demanded, grasping for the weapon. Her voice betrayed her years at school in Boston.

He held the rifle away from her and smiled. From the line of her chin and her deep brown eyes, it was clear to him that this was his father's daughter. "Not so fast, little sister," he said in a Texas drawl. "First, tell me why you tried to kill me."

She shook her head vigorously. "I did not try to kill you, only scare you off. I placed that bullet exactly where I wanted it. You've no right to trespass on this land." Her eyes narrowed as she scrutinized him. His trail-worn clothes and stubbled chin did not show him at his best. "Go tell your boss that I'm willing to sell the ranch if it becomes mine. There's no need to send a thug like you to persuade me. The sooner I get back to civilization the better."

He stared at her with admiration. "You really that good a shot?"

She again reached for the Winchester. "May I?"

He weighed her request and decided he could

trust her. She pointed to a cottonwood across the river. "See that small branch jutting upwards?"

With liquid motion he drew his six-gun and fired, clipping the branch off two inches above the main branch. "That one?" he asked.

"That one," she said, cutting off the rest of the branch with a well-placed rifle bullet.

"Pretty fancy shooting for a young girl," he said. "What are you, about thirteen?"

She laughed and he liked the music of it. "I suppose I do look like a child in this getup. If I were in my own clothes, you'd see that I'm a woman of twenty-one years."

His eyebrows came together in puzzlement. "Impossible! It's plain you're my sister, but you weren't even born when I left home fourteen years ago."

Her eyes went wide. "You're . . . you're the prodigal son we've been expecting? It's about time you got here. Judge Parker was asking about you at church on Sunday. He can't settle Papa's estate without you."

While she was talking, Jim puzzled over who she could be. "If you're not my half-sister, who are you?"

"Betsy Pinchot Lattimore," she said, extending her small, well-shaped hand. "I was eight when my mother married your father and we moved here from San Francisco. Mama caught a fever and died two years ago and, as you probably know, your father died three months ago after a fall from his horse. Now that you know who I am, tell me for sure who you are. You don't favor my stepfather in the least."

He shrugged. "Be that as it may, I truly am the prodigal son, Jim Lattimore."

She looked at him suspiciously. "Can you prove it?" He reached into his shirt pocket and handed her a crumpled letter. She glanced at the name and address and handed it back to him. "I hope you haven't come all the way from Texas expecting to inherit the ranch. You broke your father's heart when you ran off." At the mention of the rift between him and his father, she could see the hurt in his eyes and immediately regretted her words. "I'm sorry. I had no right to say that.

It's just that I was hardly off the train from Boston when Colonel Watson was trying to get the ranch from me. I thought that you too—"

"Don't worry," he said evenly. "I have no expectations. I'm here to settle things up, and then I'll be on my way. Now tell me, why are you here all alone. Where are the hands?"

Betsy sighed. "Come on inside and I'll explain." He followed her into the house and took a seat at the kitchen table. "Would you like some tea?"

"Coffee if you have it."

She hesitated. "Yes. I have it."

While she was making the coffee, he surveyed the room. "Except for the fancy curtains and pictures on the walls, it hasn't changed much."

"No it hasn't. If I were staying, I'd make some improvements. But, like you, as soon as things are settled I'll be gone—back to Boston where I've spent the last five years. By the way, I don't always dress like this. My Boston clothes are just not suitable for working around the ranch and with all the help gone . . ." she let the sentence dangle. "Here's your coffee."

He nodded his thanks and she turned back to the stove. Taking a huge swallow, he gulped and his lips puckered. She turned in time to see the grimace on his face.

"That bad?" she asked.

He nodded slowly. "I've drunk coffee from Mexico to Canada and I can truthfully say this is the worst cup I've ever tasted. Didn't your mother teach you how?"

She smiled and shook her head. "She didn't know how either. We brought our Chinese cook from San Francisco. After your father died, Ling Yee went back to San Francisco to fetch a mail-order-bride. He's not returned."

"I assume you attended school back in Boston. Didn't they teach you how to cook?"

She shook her head. "Of course not. Cooking is not part of finishing school. I studied such things as French, elocution, deportment, dancing, piano, needlepoint—you know, all the important things."

He smiled. "Did you learn anything at all that

might be helpful on a ranch?"

Her eyebrows came together as she thought about the question. "Well, we did have equestrian classes, but I knew how to ride before I went east. Your father taught me how to ride and shoot."

He thought on this for a moment and then remembered that she was going to tell him about why she was alone at the ranch. "So why are you all alone?"

She sighed and sat down across from him, a cup of tea in her hands. "By the time I got here from Boston all the help had gone, except for Gabe Conklin—"

"He's still around? I thought he'd have drunk himself to death by now."

"Actually, he's probably off on a drunk right now. He went to town three days ago and hasn't returned. He's done that twice before and I warned him that if he did it again he'd be dismissed. The other hands were either scared off by Colonel Watson or hired by him. The colonel covets this ranch most vehemently."

"Who is this Watson? He wasn't here when I left."

"He came to the territory about the same time as Mama and I. Through buying up the ranches of failed homesteaders, he's quilted together an empire. I suspect he's had something to do with some of the ranchers failing. He appears to have great influence with the bank and the railroad. He's unbending in his desire to get the Double 'L.'"

Jim nodded. "It's one of the best ranches in Wyoming. How many head are there now?"

She shook her head. "I don't really know. Gabe was looking after them. All I've been doing is feeding the chickens and trying to milk the cow and such things. Before he disappeared, Gabe said the cattle needed to be moved to the higher pasture." She looked at him expectantly. "Do you suppose you could help me do that? We could probably get old Ben as well."

"Old Ben?"

"He's a kind of hermit who lives on the ranch up near the Beaver Ponds. He survives on hunting and trapping. I don't know much about him. I understand he used to work here but left when his wife and child died. He returned about five years ago a broken man. Papa allowed him to build a cabin and live on the ranch."

"I know where the ponds are." He thought for a minute before adding, "all right. I'll help move the cattle after I see Judge Parker."

"You won't be able to see him until at least Saturday. He's in Laramie for the week."

Jim considered this. "Okay, today's Tuesday. I'm yours for the next three days. We'll start the drive tomorrow. Once I get settled I'll ride up to the ponds and recruit the trapper. Where would you like me to put my gear?"

Betsy hesitated before answering and he could see a slight blush on her pretty cheeks. "If you don't mind, it would be more seemly if you stayed in the bunkhouse—we not being blood relations and all."

He smiled. "I don't mind, Betsy. I've spent a lot of years in bunkhouses."

When he opened the bunkhouse door, he took a

step back at the overpowering stench. He was sitting on the steps when Betsy approached, laden with clean bedding.

"Is it not to your liking?" she asked. He took the bedding from her and motioned with his head towards the bunkhouse door. She stuck her head in. "Oh, my. I see what you mean. If you start hauling out the refuse, I'll get a bucket and some lye soap."

For the next two hours they cleaned out the bunkhouse. Jim admired his newfound stepsister's energy and willingness to pitch in despite her Boston schooling. They finished the job by refilling the mattresses with fresh straw.

"There," she said with satisfaction. "It's not quite up to Boston standards, but much better than before. Would you like something to eat before you go see Ben?"

He thought about the coffee. "No thanks. I have some grub in my saddlebag. How 'bout I make supper when I get back. I'm a fair hand in the kitchen."

2

Jim's heart sang as he rode across the valley, following Beaver Creek towards the mountains. This was always his favorite time of year. The aroma of new growth, the music of the birds and the warmth of the sun all conspired to happiness. His mind went back to the last time he'd been up at the Beaver Ponds and he recalled with pleasure the many trout he'd caught. Finding that he had such a pretty and pleasant stepsister also added to his good mood. It was nice to know that he was no longer alone in the world.

A cacophony interrupted his reverie. Urging Toby to a gallop, he soon reached the scene of the disturbance. Across the creek, several horsemen had lassoed an old man with silver hair and flowing beard. The cowboys were pulling him this way and that while yelling at the top of their lungs. The bound man was silent. Jim spurred Toby across the creek, leapt to the ground and went to the old man. The cowboys fell silent. Jim pulled a clasp knife out of his pocket and opened it. "Slacken those lariats, boys, or they'll be short a few feet," he said.

Four of the cowboys obeyed, and Jim slipped the ropes off the captive. The fifth, however, kept the lasso taut. "Cut that rope," he growled, "and you're a dead man."

Jim quickly switched the knife from his right hand to his left, freeing his gun hand. With one eye on his adversary, he moved forward to cut the rope. The cowboy went for his gun, but not fast enough. In a flash he screamed in pain as a bullet creased the back of his hand. Jim slowly holstered his gun and cut the lariat.

At that moment a stocky man with military bearing rode onto the scene. "What's going on here?"

he demanded.

"We was jist havin' a little fun with the half-wit, colonel," said one of the cowboys, "when this jasper butts in."

The military man stared at the man dripping blood. "Did you draw first, Jenkins?" The cowboy seemed to have lost his tongue. "Obviously, you did. You know the rule. No violence. You're through! Pick up your pay at the office. The rest of you men get back to work. I'm not paying you to harass old men." He turned to Jim. "What are you doing on my land, stranger?" he asked with surface cordiality.

"Crossed the creek to help the old timer," Jim said evenly.

Through covetous eyes, the man glanced across the creek before accepting Jim's answer with a curt nod. He turned his attention to the old man. "What were you doing here, Watters? You've been warned to stay off my property." Ben made no reply. "There's a dying deer up the trail aways. Were you following it?" Ben nodded. "All right, go fetch it and from now on stay off my land if you know what's good for you."

Ben picked up an old single shot rifle from the ground and went after the deer. The military man dismounted and put out his hand to Jim. "Colonel Watson," he said, the surface cordiality returning. "I don't believe I've had the pleasure."

Jim shook his hand. "Jim Lattimore. I'm sure you knew my father."

Colonel Watson nodded. "Of course. He was a good man, even though he stubbornly refused to sell out to me. I admire a man that stands up to me. But perhaps you'll be more accommodating. That is, if the ranch falls to you."

"I doubt it will, seeing I deserted my father years ago. My stepsister has the greater claim."

The colonel slowly nodded and briefly studied the Texan. "Obviously you can handle yourself, Mr. Lattimore. Since I just fired my foreman, how'd you like to work for me?"

Jim glanced across the creek. "Things are a mite unsettled right now, Colonel. Let me get back to you on that."

"Of course. Take your time." With that the

older man re-mounted and was gone.

A few minutes later, Ben returned with a young buck across his shoulders. Jim offered to carry the deer across his saddle and the old man nodded his acceptance. As the two men walked to the Beaver Ponds in silence, Jim wondered about his companion. Although stooped with age and hard living, he looked to be over six feet. His hair and beard hadn't been cut in years. His leathery skin testified to his years outdoors.

A man playing solitaire outside a rude cabin looked up as Jim and Ben approached. He stood up and, despite the intervening years, Jim recognized the short, bald man with the ruddy complexion as the missing Gabe Tanner.

As they got closer to the cabin, the aroma of venison stew reminded Jim that he was starving. He had turned down Betsy's offer of lunch and had not delved into his saddlebags. He hoped that he would be invited to share the trapper's table and was not disappointed. After introductions, the three of them, Ben Watters, Gabe Tanner and Jim, sat around a puncheon table and ate their fill of the savory stew.

"So you see, Mr. Lattimore," Gabe said as they finished eating, "it's those Bar 'W' boys what got me drunk. I guess they wanted to keep me away from the ranch so's Miss Betsy wouldn't have no help and be forced t'sell out to the colonel. D'ya think you could put in a good word fer me to Miss Betsy?"

Jim nodded. "Call me Jim. I'll smooth things with Miss Lattimore. We need you for the drive to the upper pasture. Would you like to come, too, Ben?"

Ben shook his head, no.

"You up fer some fishin' afore we go back, Jim?" Gabe asked.

Jim hesitated. His mind went back to the many happy hours he'd spent with his father at the Beaver Ponds before the rift. "We should get back—but maybe an hour or so wouldn't hurt."

In two hours they each had a string of trout. Ben wrapped the fish in ice from the icehouse and Jim and Gabe were soon on their way.

"Too bad Ben didn't come along. We could have used him," Jim said.

"He don't cotton much to company."

"Doesn't he talk at all?"

"A word now and then. He was half-dead when he showed up at the ranch. He ain't never recovered proper. Some folks thinks he's tetched."

"Miss Lattimore said he used to work for my father."

Gabe nodded. "He started to work for your pa years ago when they was both bachelors. He become your pa's foreman and best friend. They both married at the same time, and their wives both got in the family way at the same time. But when it come time for the gals to give birth, your ma bore you with nary a hitch. But Mrs. Watters ran into a heap o' trouble. Her and the infant died. Ben just about went off his haid. He turned to drink and soon left the valley. Like I said, a few years ago he showed up again. Your pa took him in and helped him build the cabin." Gabe paused for a moment before adding, "Ben's all right. Like I said, he don't cotton to company, but he took me in when I sobered up. I didn't have nowhere else to go."

It was after dark when Jim and Gabe got back

to the ranch buildings. An upstairs light was showing in the main house. Jim, supposing that Betsy had retired, decided not to disturb her. He and Gabe went right to the bunkhouse and to bed. For several hours Jim tossed and turned on the straw mattress. Finally, he got up and went outside to get a drink from the pump. The upstairs light was still on. *She must be doing something awful important*, he thought.

Next morning Jim awoke to the noise of Gabe closing the bunkhouse door. Jim arose and looked out the window. Gabe was heading for the house. *Looks like Gabe's going to cook breakfast. I hope he knows how to make a good cup of coffee.*

After washing at the pump and putting on his other shirt, Jim headed for the house. Betsy met him on the porch. "Ah, there you are, brother," she said. "I was coming to get you." Jim stared at her with unabashed admiration. She reminded him of a dancer he had once known in Amarillo. The man's shirt and dungarees had been taken in and no longer disguised her shapely figure. "So that's what you were doing late into the night," he said. Betsy stared at him innocently. "Your clothes. No one would mistake you for a thirteen-year-old this morning!"

Betsy smiled and her cheeks colored. "I'll take that as a compliment. Come along. Gabe has prepared breakfast. I'm told he makes a good cup of coffee."

After breakfast the three of them mounted up and began rounding up the cattle. Betsy proved that she could ride well and, although she knew little about herding cattle, she was a quick learner. By ten o'clock they had rounded up the herd and were on their way towards the mountains. The sun was overhead when they stopped in a pretty valley for lunch.

"Will you teach me how to use a lariat, Jim?" Betsy asked, as they were finishing up the meal.

Jim looked up at the sun. "Perhaps for a few minutes. Then we'd best be moving."

"I'll clean up," Gabe said.

Jim looked around. "We'll use that stump," he said.

He lassoed the stump several times to show her how. She tried several times with no success.

She sighed. "I just can't seem to get the knack

of it."

"You ain't holding it proper. Let me show you." Putting his arms around her, he placed her hands on the rope. He hadn't been this close to a woman in a long time, and the hint of flowers from her hair both fascinated him and scared him. "Maybe we'll try this another time," he said abruptly. "We ought to be going."

Over the next three days Jim couldn't have been happier. It was good to be back on the ranch he had loved as a boy. The spring weather was perfect and he was doing what he loved to do. But above all, he enjoyed his two companions. Gabe was full of humorous stories and the music in Betsy's laughter awoke something that had lain dormant in his heart for a long time. He had come to accept the loneliness of the past five years as his lot in life. Now he began to live again.

"Tell me, Jim," Betsy said, as the three of them sat around the campfire on Thursday evening, their last day on the trail. "How come some Texas girl hasn't roped you by now?"

Jim smiled. "You're talking like a rancher's daughter. What would your elocution teacher say?" He then grew serious and looked off into space, remembering. "A pretty Galveston gal did rope me. Susanna Carmady. We had less than a year together before yellow fever took her. Since then I haven't been very good company."

Betsy touched his arm. "I'm so sorry, Jim. I can see you loved her very much."

He nodded. "That I did. It seems the people I love always leave me, Ma, Susie—or I leave them."

"Why did you run off so young?" Betsy asked. "If you care to talk about it."

Jim sighed and smiled wryly. "It seems so silly when I look back on it. It was all over a horse, a black stallion Pa bought at an auction. The thing was half-wild, but Pa loved that animal. Not long after Ma died it got out of the corral and took off. Pa blamed me for not latching the corral gate proper. We took off after it and found it on the ground all lathered up. Its front leg was broke, got caught in a gopher hole. Pa had to shoot it. When we got back to the house he gave me a tongue-lashing. Well, I'd had enough. Ever since Ma died, he'd been impossible to live with. That night I cleared out and joined a bunch of Texas drovers heading home. I was big for my age and they believed me when I told them I was sixteen. They took me on as a cook's helper. That's where I learned to cook."

A pall fell over the camp when Jim stopped talking. For a few minutes no one spoke.

"Speakin' of horses," Gabe said, breaking the silence. "A cowpoke called Slim went to a dealer to buy a horse. He picked one out, and the dealer says a preacher used to own it. The only thing was, to get it goin' y'had to say 'church,' to get it gallopin' y'had to say 'Praise the Lord' and to stop it y'had to say 'Amen.' Well, Slim, he bought the nag and got on. He says 'church' and off it went. When he got out of town, he says 'Praise the Lord" and the beast took off like lightnin'. Poor Slim hung on fer dear life, yelling 'Whoa! Whoa! Stop you stupid horse, stop!" Well the more he yelled the faster it went. When Slim saw they was headin' fer a cliff, he panicked and screamed, "Please, God, stop this horse! Please! Amen.' Well, that ol' horse stopped dead, right at the edge of the cliff. Slim breathed a sigh of relief and thankfulness and says, 'Praise the Lord!'"

Jim and Betsy broke into laughter and the evening ended on a cheerful note.

3

As Jim rode along with Betsy and Gabe the next day he was sorry that their excursion was over. He had thoroughly enjoyed the three days during which most of his thoughts were on the present. Now, as they approached the ranch house, he wondered what the future might hold.

"Thanks for all your help, Jim," Betsy said, guiding her horse alongside his. "We couldn't have done it without you."

"My pleasure, Betsy. Regardless of what Judge Parker has to say, I'd be happy to stick around until the ranch is in good shape again."

She gave him an appreciative smile. "I'd like that very much—oh, it looks like we have company."

Jim's eyes turned from Betsy and rested on a buggy sitting in the yard.

"There you are, Betsy," said a buxom woman of indeterminable age as she climbed down from the buggy. "I was wondering what happened to you. I was just about ready to leave. And who is this handsome stranger?"

"My stepbrother, Jim Lattimore. Jim, this is Mrs. Flora Fenwick—"

"Widow Fenwick," said the woman quickly, "but call me Flora, everybody does. Pleased to meet you, Mr. Lattimore. May I call you Jim?" Jim nodded. Without taking her eyes off him, Flora continued: "I'm out and about inviting folks to a dance tomorrow night at the church hall. Won't you come, Jim?"

Jim rubbed his three days' growth of beard and slowly shook his head. "Sorry, Flora, but I left my dancing duds in Texas." With a motion of his hands he indicated the clothes he was wearing. "These're all

I've got."

Betsy, who had stood by bemused at Flora's brashness, spoke up. "I'm sure I could find you some clothes, Jim." Turning to Flora she said. "I suppose I'm invited, too?"

"Of course, dear," Flora said. "I'll expect you both—and Gabe too—at seven sharp." With that she climbed back into the buggy. After a long, appraising glance at Jim, she cracked the whip and was gone.

Betsy grinned at Jim. "Well, what do you think of Widow Fenwick?"

Jim's eyebrows came together, and he feigned great thought. "A fine figure of a woman," he finally said, "even if she is a little long in the tooth."

Betsy laughed. "Come. Light the stove for me and I'll draw you a bath."

"I'll light the stove, but I think I'll go up to my old swimming hole to wash up."

"As you wish."

Jim had finished lighting the stove when Betsy came downstairs carrying a towel, soap, and a small bottle. "You'll need these," she said.

Jim thanked her and studied the bottle. "What's this?"

"Liquid soap. It's for washing your hair. In Boston we call it shampooing."

"Will it make my hair smell as good as yours?" Betsy nodded and Jim handed back the bottle. "Thanks all the same. Toby'd throw me if I smelled as pretty as you!"

"This should fit you," Betsy said after breakfast next morning, showing Jim a three-piece, black suit. "I found it at the back of the upstairs closet. I'll air it out to get rid of the mothball smell."

Jim studied the suit. "These ain't Pa's clothes. They're for a taller man. I wonder whose they are?"

"I don't know," Betsy said. "Maybe somebody that worked on the ranch in the past left them. Here, try on the coat."

It fit perfectly. Later, while dressing for the dance, Jim again wondered who had left it. While Gabe went to get the wagon, Jim walked over to the house for Betsy. She wasn't ready yet, so he sat down at the kitchen table and began nervously tapping his fingers. He wondered why he felt so strange, almost fearful. Why should he who had braved swollen rivers, cattle stampedes and prairie fires unflinchingly, be suddenly anxious now? After all, he was only taking his sister to a dance.

Betsy entered the room carrying her cloak. Jim's heart skipped a beat and he leapt to his feet. In her fashionable Boston gown, she was stunningly beautiful.

"You don't think I'm over-dressed, do you?" she asked, handing him her cloak.

Jim didn't answer right away. Her closeness and intoxicating aroma temporarily tied his tongue. He took the hooded garment and helped her on with it. "No. You're not over-dressed," he finally stammered. "You'll be the belle of the ball."

"Thank you, Jim," she said, politely ignoring his obvious discomfiture. "You look very handsome in that suit. Sorry it still smells a little of mothballs. However, that won't keep Flora Fenwick away. She'll be all over you. If you need me to rescue you, just tell her that you promised me a dance."

Betsy was right. Flora Fenwick moved in for the kill the moment Jim entered the hall. After several dances with her, Jim was about to use Betsy's escape line, but she was dancing with a handsome young man. They seemed to know each other. Jim resisted the urge to dump Flora and cut in. He was gazing around for a more dignified escape when a distinguished man entered the hall.

"Is that Judge Parker?" he asked Flora.

"It is."

"In that case, will you excuse me? I have some very important business with him."

Flora frowned. "Only if you promise to return to me when you're finished your business."

Jim hedged. "If it isn't too late." He quickly divested himself of Flora and walked over to the judge. "Judge Parker, I'm Jim Lattimore."

"Ah, Mr. Lattimore. You've finally arrived from Texas. Welcome. Can I see you in my office on Monday morning?"

"Would it be possible to see you now, sir?" Jim

glanced toward Flora, who smiled and waved at him.

The judge followed Jim's glance and took the situation in. "Ah," he said. "You need rescuing from our Flora. All right, let's go. It's only a short buggy ride to my office."

4

The office was on the main street of Cheyenne Springs. When they were both seated, the judge said, "Your father's will is not extensive. The only beneficiaries are you and your half-sister—"

"You mean stepsister, don't you, Judge?"

The judge shook his head. "No. Betsy is your father's daughter."

Jim's mind went back to his first meeting with Betsy and for some reason his heart sank.

The judge explained that twenty-two years earlier, Larry Lattimore was part of a delegation of ranchers who had gone to San Francisco to meet with a syndicate proposing to broker Wyoming stock to the Orient. At that time most Wyoming cattle were shipped east to Chicago. The syndicate proposed shipping the cattle to the West Coast instead. The scheme never succeeded, but the cream of San Francisco society feted the Wyoming delegates. At one party, Larry met a ballet dancer, Darla Pinchot. It was an odd match, the beautiful, refined Miss Pinchot and the rugged Wyoming rancher; but they became passionately en-amored of each other. When it came time for Larry to return home, they had to make a hard decision. Darla didn't want to leave the stage just as she was reaching her prime as a dancer, and Larry would not desert his wife and son. They decided to part and never see each other again. When Larry returned home he confessed his affair to his wife. Eventually, she forgave him.

The judge stopped at this point in his narration and studied Jim. "Although your mother forgave him, I don't think he ever forgave himself. One cannot break God's laws with impunity. Your father was never the same afterwards."

"Don't I know it," Jim said. "He became even worse after Ma died."

The judge nodded. "After she died and you ran off to Texas, your father re-established communication with Miss Pinchot. He was shocked to discover that she had borne his child."

"Betsy!" Jim exclaimed. "I figured the first time I saw her that she was my father's daughter."

The judge nodded. "Yes. To make a long story short, your father proposed marriage; Darla accepted and she and Betsy moved here. I'd like to say it was a happy marriage, but Darla never did become reconciled to the rough life in cow country. You know what they say; this is 'a great country for men, but hell on women and horses!' The only bright light in your father's life was Betsy. He loved that girl to distraction."

"I wonder why they never told Betsy that she is their natural child?"

The judge thought about the question for a moment. "I don't know. I suppose it had something to do with the stigma of being born out of wedlock." The judge paused for a moment. "Now, to your father's will. The whole estate has been left jointly to you and Betsy. I'll help you work out the details. Your father recognized that Betsy liked the East and indicated to me that if she wanted to live there permanently, he had no objections. In fact, he felt that she would be happier there. Well, son, that's about it. You can share all this with Betsy, and as soon as you've both had time to think things over, come and see me and we'll settle the details. Any questions?"

Jim had no questions. He should have been happy with the outcome of the meeting. After all, he had just inherited half of the ranch he loved. But instead he felt as if he'd been kicked in the stomach by a mule. He felt that something precious had slipped from his grasp, and the nagging pain in the pit of his stomach would not go away. On his return to the dance, Flora ambushed him, and he had no will to fend her off. Betsy was still keeping company with the handsome young man, and that further soured Jim's evening.

"We didn't get our dance," Betsy said to Jim

on their way home. He was driving, she was sitting beside him and Gabe was asleep in the back.

"No. We didn't," he said acidly.

For a while neither of them spoke. "You spent a lot of time with Flora Fenwick," she said, breaking the silence. "I was surprised. Also, you disappeared for awhile."

He kept looking straight ahead. "I could hardly spend time with you since you were with some fellow all evening."

She ignored the accusation in his voice. "Aaron Watson," she said, matter-of-factly. "We've been friends ever since I moved here. He just returned from Ann Arbor, Michigan where he's been attending college. He's been offered a teaching position there, but his father insists he stay here and learn to be a rancher." Jim didn't respond, and for another long time they traveled in silence. "It's a little chilly tonight," she finally added.

"There's a blanket under the seat." He tried to say this as evenly as possible, but Betsy was well aware that he was angry about something.

She decided to confront him. "Have I said or done something to offend you, Jim?"

He couldn't bear to hear the hurt in her voice. "No, Betsy you haven't. I'm sorry for being an old grump. I'll pull over. I have something to tell you."

He halted the wagon, got the blanket from under the seat and put it around her shoulders, all without speaking.

"You look so serious," she said. "What ever can it be?"

"Do you remember when we first met, I was sure that you were my half-sister?"

"Yes. I'm used to hearing that I resembled Papa. People often pointed it out. But as I explained, I was eight when my mother married your father."

"It was not just a resemblance. Larry Lattimore is your father."

Betsy gasped and her hands went to her open mouth. "How could that be?"

Jim told her all that he had learned from Judge Parker. When he was finished, neither of them spoke for a few moments. Except for Gabe's snoring all was quiet. Betsy was the first to speak. "So we really are brother and sister. I'm glad Papa left you half the ranch. I know how much you love it. Will you stay now and run it?"

"I think I will."

"Good. I'm glad that Colonel Watson won't get it."

"Have you any idea what you'll do?"

"Go back to Boston, I suppose."

"I'll miss you, but I'm sure it will be for the best. Ranch life is hard on women."

Again they fell silent. Then Betsy remembered something. "Aaron Watson asked if it would be all right to call on me. There's some fancy do at the Bar 'W' next Saturday night. The colonel is hosting some big-wigs from the east. Aaron has asked me to go. I told him I'd have to check with you."

For some reason this irritated Jim. "With me? You're a grown woman. You don't need my permission."

"I know, but you are my big brother. I've never had a brother before and am not sure of the protocol."

"It's fine with me if he comes calling," Jim lied. "What's he like?"

"He's a good man, not overbearing like his father. In fact, one of his failings is that he allows his father to dominate him. He didn't really want to come home from college, but his father commanded him to do so."

"Well, I'll talk to him when he comes calling, and see if he's good enough for my little sister."

A week later Jim was finishing up the dinner dishes when he heard Aaron Watson's buggy stop in front of the house. Gabe was doing the evening chores and Betsy was getting ready for the Saturday night do at the Bar "W." Jim quickly put away the dish towel and sat down at the kitchen table. Betsy's caller was soon sitting across from him.

"You've given up your studies?" Jim asked.

"Yes, sir.

"No need to call me 'sir.' I'm not that much older than you. You can call me Jim. How old are you?"

"Twenty-one, sir . . . I mean, Jim. The same as Betsy."

"I probably look older, but I'm only twenty-eight. What are your intentions toward Betsy?"

"Strictly honorable. She's one of the nicest girls I know."

Jim's eyes narrowed. "You know lots of girls? Did you leave a sweetheart at college?" Aaron looked up nervously, and he became slightly flushed. He hesitated. "It's not a very difficult question," Jim added.

"In a manner of speaking. That is, I had a . . . a friend, Jenny Roberts, but she broke off our relationship."

Jim relished Aaron's discomfiture. "Why did she do that?"

Again Aaron hesitated. "She wanted me to take a teaching position at the college and my father didn't want me to."

"What did you want to do?"

Aaron avoided the question. "He is my father and I'm his only heir."

Jim was about to say that Aaron hadn't answered the question when Betsy entered the room and rescued her suitor. Aaron breathed a sigh of relief and leapt to his feet. After they had gone, Jim sat back down at the table and began drumming his fingers. *Tomorrow, I'll pack some things and ride fence for a few days. No, tomorrow's Sunday. Betsy'll expect me to go to church with her. Well, Monday, then.*

5

Over the next months Jim threw himself into rebuilding the ranch. Although loath to do it, he took out a mortgage at the bank to provide the capital needed to build up the stock, buy new equipment and hire new hands. He and Betsy had firmly turned down Colonel Watson's offer to buy the ranch.

As the summer went by, Jim and Betsy eased into what could pass for a normal sibling relationship. In July, Betsy received a letter offering her a position at her alma mater, Miss Sorsby's School for Young Ladies. She discussed it with Jim and decided to accept it. She would be heading east in late August. Jim would be sad to see her go, but he knew it was for the best.

In the meantime, Aaron Watson continued courting her. He panicked when he learned that Betsy had accepted the teaching position. One day in mid-August Jim was fixing a fence when Aaron rode up and tethered his horse. The younger man stood nervously by while Jim finished what he was doing.

"Done," Jim said, slipping off his heavy gloves and shaking hands with Aaron. "What can I do for you, Aaron?"

Aaron hesitated and took a deep breath. "I'll get right to the point, Jim. I want your permission to marry Betsy."

Jim's jaw dropped. "Marry Betsy? Why, you know she's going east in two weeks. It's all set."

"I know. That's why I have to act fast. Will you give us your blessing?"

Jim methodically took a red bandanna from his pocket and wiped his brow. "How does Betsy feel about it?"

"I think she'll agree if you approve. She sets great store by you."

Jim slowly nodded. "I hope you know Betsy's happiness is my only concern, Aaron. Where would you live if you wed?"

"At the Bar 'W.' Pa has given up on my being a rancher, but he thinks he can teach me the business end of things. He wants me to get married and settle down. He approves of Betsy."

This last sentence was like a red flag to a bull. "Hold on, Aaron. Is it your father or you that wants this marriage?"

Aaron knew he had made a gaff and started back peddling. "Me, of course. All I'm saying is that my father has given us his blessing. Now I'm asking for yours."

Jim pursed his lips and slowly nodded. "Let me study on it for a bit. I'll talk to Betsy and get her feelings."

That evening he did talk with Betsy. "If I give my blessing," Jim said, "will you accept his proposal?"

Betsy thought for a moment and then slowly nodded. "We've known each other for years and I truly believe we love each other. Oh, it's not the passionate love of romantic novels, but we like to do things together and he's devoted to me."

"Strange that he didn't mention he loved you when he asked for your hand," Jim said reflectively. "I would have thought that would have been the first thing he should have said."

Betsy suddenly became agitated. "Jim, if you can't give us your blessing just say so. We're of age and can get married without it. Aaron's asking you was merely a sign of respect."

Jim looked hurt. "Of course I'll give you my blessing. I was just trying to fulfill my role as your elder brother, and I'm the first to admit I'm not very good at it."

Betsy's face softened, and she threw her arms around him. "You're the best big brother in the world."

Over the next two weeks the upcoming marriage of Betsy Lattimore and Aaron Watson was the talk of the territory. Colonel Watson spared no expense in the preparations, even engaging a chef, Monsieur Philipe Gagnon from Cheyenne, to oversee the wedding feast.

The closer the wedding day came, the more withdrawn and taciturn Jim became. Even though he didn't really want to participate in the preparations, he thought he ought to. But there was little for him to do. Colonel Watson had taken complete control. As Mrs. Watson was semi-invalid, the colonel had hired Flora Fenwick, who had some experience with weddings since she'd buried two husbands, to look after the feminine side of things. So it was that the day before the wedding, Flora visited the ranch. She summoned Jim from the corral to see Betsy in her wedding dress. He reluctantly left what he was doing and followed Flora into the ranch house. Flora sat him in a chair and called for the bride. When Betsy entered the room in a flounced, Indian Muslin gown, Jim's heart sank. Despite his brave front, he could not become reconciled to her marrying Aaron—or anyone for that matter. For her sake, however, he went through the motions of congratulating both women on the choice of the gown. He couldn't wait to get out of the house.

Flora insisted that Betsy stay in town at Flora's place that night.

"Don't forget, Reverend Green wants you at the church by eleven sharp," Flora said to Jim as the two women got into Flora's buggy. "The wedding's at noon."

"I won't forget," Jim said.

As the buggy drove away, Jim smiled and waved, but his stomach was churning. That night was the longest of his life. Some months earlier, when the new hands had been hired, he had moved into his father and mother's old room in the main house. Despite the comfortable feather bed, he could not sleep. All night long he paced the floor of the empty house. By morning he had come to a decision: he would give his half of the ranch to Betsy and Aaron as a wedding present and he would return to Texas.

6

Leaving a note on the kitchen table to that effect, he saddled Toby, strapped on his few possessions and headed up Beaver Creek, taking the long way around so as not to run into anyone who might ask him questions. He had a mind to say goodbye to Ben, but he decided against it.

Fate, however, intervened. Not far from the Beaver Ponds, he spied Ben heading for his cabin. Jim waved to the old man and continued riding. To Jim's surprise, Ben waved him over. Not wanting to offend Ben, Jim reluctantly complied. Dismounting near the cabin, he tethered Toby, sat on the porch in a chair made of branches and waited for Ben. He wondered how they were going to communicate since Gabe had done all of the talking on Jim's last visit to Ben's cabin.

Ben joined Jim on the porch and sat on another branch chair. The old man smiled at Jim and nodded. Jim smiled back. Suddenly the old man surprised Jim by talking a stream of words.

"I have a strange tale to tell, Jim. Strange but true. Twenty-eight years ago I was the foreman here on the ranch. I was married to a wonderful woman, Sarah. Life couldn't of been better. But one night tragedy struck. Both Sarah and Celia Lattimore was delivered of baby boys. Sarah died giving birth and Celia's child only lived a few hours. When Doc Ames told me Sarah died, I went out of my head. She was the world to me. He asked what he should do about my son, and I told him I didn't care. I took off to Cheyenne Springs and drunk myself unconscious. Days later I returned to the ranch and found out that Doc had done the sensible thing. He'd given my boy—you, son—to Celia to raise. I accepted this, but my heart was broke."

Jim was sitting forward in his chair staring into Ben's face. "You mean, you're . . . you're my father? Does anyone else know?"

Ben shook his head. "The only ones that knowed was Larry, Celia, and Doc Ames, all dead now." Ben looked apologetic. "I'm sorry, son. It must be an awful shock learning I'm your pa."

Jim shook his head. "Of course not. If you're my father, you're my father. But why didn't you tell me this when I was first here?"

Ben hung his head and seemed unable to answer. Finally, he looked up sheepishly and said, "I guess for selfish reasons, both for me and for you. If the word gets out that you're not really Larry's son, your claim to the ranch could be contested and the place could end up in Watson's hands. If that happened, I'd be out on my ear. He wouldn't tolerate me staying here in the cabin."

Jim digested this information before saying, "You could be right. But surely the Lattimores must have legally adopted me. Being a son by adoption is just as valid as being a natural son."

Ben shrugged. "Maybe they did. I don't know." He paused for a moment before asking, "Gabe says Miss Lattimore's marrying the Watson boy. Is that true?"

Jim nodded. "Yes. Today at noon."

Ben shook his head and gave a rueful smile. "So Watson's got half the ranch already. It won't be long before he has it all." He nodded towards Jim's laden horse. "You going somewheres?"

Jim also glanced at Toby. "Yes. Back to Texas."

Ben leaned forward and gripped Jim's arm. Jim was surprised at the strength of the old man's fingers. "Don't do it, son. You can't run away from life. I know. I've spent most all my life running away, first in drink and then in prospecting. Fifteen years I spent wandering through Utah, Nevada and Idaho looking for the big strike. And when I finally made a strike up in the Idaho panhandle, some road agents snatched it from me and left me for dead. Somehow I made it back to here and Larry took me in. You were born on this ranch, son. This is your home. Don't run away again. Stay and fight."

Jim weighed his father's words and it suddenly dawned on him that in making the noble gesture of giving his half of the ranch to Betsy, he was playing into Watson's hands. The Double "L" would soon be quilted onto the Bar "W" empire. Well, not if he could help it. "Thanks . . . Ben . . . Pa."

Ben smiled. "Ben's good enough. I've never been a real pa to you, and it's too late to start. All I can do for you is urge you to stand your ground. Fight for what's yours."

As Jim rode towards Cheyenne Springs, his mind was in turmoil. Could he believe the old man? All those who could corroborate his story were dead. And even if he were Ben's son, how did that change things? Ben told him to fight, but for what? If he were not Larry Lattimore's son, then Betsy had a full right to the ranch and it was her business what she did with it.

As for Betsy herself, he finally admitted to

himself that he loved her; but what could he do about it? They may not be blood relations, but she was his stepsister and society forbade such a relationship. He looked up at the sun and determined that it was noon. It was too late anyway. By now Betsy and Aaron would be married. Despite his newfound father's advice, Jim concluded that the best thing for all concerned would be for him to return to Texas.

Nevertheless, Toby continued on towards Cheyenne Springs. When Jim got to the edge of town, guests were streaming out of the church. Curiously, they looked as if they had just witnessed a funeral rather than a wedding. Jim dismounted and approached one of the guests. He was about to ask why everyone looked so glum when Colonel Watson stormed out of the church. Aaron was close behind him.

The colonel turned on his son and waved a piece of paper in his face. "This debacle's cost me a small fortune," the colonel raved. "Back at the ranch is the best chef in Wyoming Territory, an army of cooks and waiters, and enough food to feed the county. If this trollop thinks she can leave you standing at the alter—"

Suddenly Aaron's face filled with anger. He leapt forward and grabbed his father by the lapels of his fashionable new suit. "How dare you call Betsy that," he yelled. "She's the sweetest girl in the territory. I'm glad she had the courage not to marry me. Doubtless she realized that you engineered this whole thing to get your greedy hands on her ranch." He raised his voice even louder. "And while I'm at it, I want everyone to know that no matter what you say, I'm going back to Michigan. I'm going to take the teaching position and beg Jenny Roberts to take me back. I should have listened to her in the first place instead of being cowed by you."

Aaron let go of his father's lapels, folded his arms, and glowered at the colonel. Spontaneous applause arose from the guests, who had observed the altercation in shocked silence. The colonel glanced around the crowd as if trying to find someone on whom to vent his anger. His eyes fell on Jim, who was clapping as hard as anyone.

"Don't you look so smug, you . . . you penniless, Texas saddle bum," the colonel sputtered. "I may not have gotten the ranch but you're not getting it either." He pointed at Jim and addressed the crowd. "This man is an impostor!" The wedding guests suddenly became quiet again. "He claims to be Larry Lattimore's son, but I have proof he's the spawn of the half-wit failure, Ben Watters."

An audible sigh came from the crowd, and Jim feigned shock. The colonel paused to let the revelation sink in. Then he yelled, "Ames, get up here." A small, bespectacled man emerged from the crowd. "Tell us what your pa's journal says."

Mr. Ames, obviously embarrassed, glanced around. "Colonel, with respect, I don't think it's appropriate—"

"Don't tell me what's appropriate," the colonel yelled. "You've been paid good money for the information. Now tell us what your pa wrote."

Mr. Ames started to tell the story that Ben had told Jim. "Louder, Ames," the colonel yelled, "I want everyone to hear!" Mr. Ames finished his report and

Watson addressed the crowd, "There's no evidence in the county records that the Lattimores ever legally adopted this man." The colonel fixed his eyes on Jim. "My advice to you is to get on your horse and go back to Texas where you came from."

All eyes turned to Jim for his reaction. To the crowd's astonishment, he was smiling. "Are you telling me, colonel," he drawled, "that I have absolutely no relationship, by blood or adoption, to the Lattimores?"

"That's exactly what I'm saying!"

Jim leapt forward and gave the colonel a bear hug. "Thank you, Colonel Watson. You've opened a gate that could lead me to becoming the happiest man in the world."

"Get off me you fool," the colonel croaked. "You're as crazy as your old man!"

Jim released the rancher and turned to the preacher. "Reverend Green, is it still possible to have a wedding today?"

The preacher hesitated. "Well, it's a mite unorthodox. Banns should be posted and—" a nudge from his wife changed his mind. "Well, I suppose we could make an exception. Where is the bride-to-be?"

"At my house," Flora Fenwick said. "Down the road, Jim. The yellow one with the white picket fence."

Jim waved his thanks to Flora. A buzz arose from the crowd and Aaron called for quiet. Jim paused to hear what he had to say. Aaron addressed the crowd. "As Pa said, we have enough food back at the ranch to feed the county. I propose that the wedding feast go ahead as planned." He turned to his father. "What say you, Pa?"

The colonel stared at his son sternly, but Jim thought he saw a hint of pride in his father's eyes. "Out of the question," he blustered. "All these people—"

"The food's only going to go to waste anyway," Aaron argued.

The colonel glanced around at the expectant crowd. "Well," he said reluctantly. "I guess it would be a shame to waste all that food. Food prepared—"

"—by the best chef in Wyoming Territory. We know!" someone yelled from the crowd, causing spontaneous laughter.

Aaron again quieted the crowd. "Then it's agreed. You're all invited to the Bar 'W' after the wedding."

As a cheer arose from the crowd, Jim mounted Toby and headed into town.

7

Betsy, still dressed in her wedding gown, answered his knock. Her red, puffy eyes went wide. "Jim!" she exclaimed, throwing herself into his arms. For a long moment she clung to him and then shyly released him. The blush on her cheeks told Jim what he needed to know.

"May I sit?" he asked.

She motioned him to a sofa in the parlor and sat beside him. "What happened to you?" she asked. "You were supposed to be at the church at eleven."

He smiled sheepishly. "I got sidetracked."

"It's just as well. It gave me time to realize that I was making a big mistake. At a few minutes to noon, I bolted. Flora drove me here and took my note back to Aaron. Although I'm awfully fond of Aaron, I don't love him. I've decided to give you my half of the ranch. All I want is a ticket back to Boston." She bowed her head and looked as if she were going to cry again.

Jim took her hand in his. "Aaron is awful fond of you as well. He stood up for you to his father. He's gone up a few notches in my estimation." He paused before adding, "Despite that, I'm mighty glad you left him at the altar."

Her eyebrows came together questioningly. "You are? Then why did you give your blessing?"

"As your brother I wanted your happiness."

"And what has changed?"

He smiled. "Everything! I found out today that I'm not your brother."

"Not my brother?" She gasped, her brow creasing with confusion. "But Judge Parker said—"

"Judge Parker said you are Larry Lattimore's

daughter and that's true. But I am not your father's son."

Bewilderment and hope filled Betsy's face.

Jim smiled, took her hand and went on to tell her all that had happened at Ben's and outside of the church. As she listened, her face turned from confusion to wonderment to outright joy. "The black suit!" she suddenly exclaimed, "the one you wore to the dance. It must have been Ben's—your father's."

"Must have been," he agreed.

She stared at him, her face full of hope. "So we're not related in any way?"

"None whatsoever. And although your father willed me half the ranch, you're the legitimate heir. It's all yours."

She shook her head. "But I want you to have it."

"There's a way we can both have it," he said, getting down on one knee and continuing to hold her hand. "Betsy, I'm just a penniless Texas saddle bum, as Colonel Watson so eloquently put it, but I love you with all my heart. Will you do me the honor of being my wife?"

Sunshine filled her face. "I will," she said, throwing her arms around his neck. Their lips came together and for a long time they clung to each other. Reluctantly, their lips parted and Jim swept her up into his arms. "Where are you taking me, sir?" she coyly asked as he carried her towards the door.

"To a wedding, my love. And afterwards to a banquet prepared by the best chef in Wyoming Territory!"

Acknowledgments

Many thanks to Dan Skoubye for including Home to Wyoming in the inaugural flight of Banda Press International's new series. Thanks also to Christy Parr for her excellent editing and to Adam Moore for the innovative cover. Finally, I appreciate very much my wife, Serenity, and her unfailing support of my passion to write.

About the Author

Home to Wyoming reflects the fascination with the West that Tom Roulstone has fostered since childhood. Born in Donegal, Ireland and raised in Glasgow, Scotland and Toronto, Ontario, Tom made his way west at the age of eighteen, moving to British Columbia. There he operated a sightseeing and touring company in the Canadian Rockies after serving a two-year mission for the Church of Jesus Christ of Latter-day Saints.

Later, Tom attended Brigham Young and Utah State Universities, earning BA and MA degrees in history and embarked on a career teaching college. Tom retired in 2000 to devote his time to writing.

Tom and his late wife, Betsy, have six children. He and his second wife, Serenity, live on Long Lake, Vancouver Island.

OTHER

ONE FLIGHT  FICTION™

BOOKS AVAILABLE:

Perceptions . . . . .0-1 hour read

Summersville . . . . .1-2 hour read

Breaking Stride . . . . .1-2 hour read

The Looking Glass Call . . . . . . .2-3 hour read

Dreamers . . . . .2-3 hour read

To give us your feedback and learn more about
One Flight Fiction™, visit us on the web.

www.OneFlightFiction.com

ONE FLIGHT  FICTION™

Banda Press International, Inc. is proud to present
ONE FLIGHT FICTION™

Perhaps you've thumbed through a magazine trying to find something to read. Or maybe you've found yourself flying from Phoenix to Dallas, with more paperwork than you can imagine awaiting your arrival. Starting a novel (that you'll never finish) just doesn't seem to cut it. Whether on a two hour flight or on a tight schedule at home; *One Flight Fiction*™ will afford you the luxury of curling up with a good book and finishing it, in less than three hours!

We look forward to filling the gap between magazines and novels; and providing you with
ONE FLIGHT FICTION™

Visit us
at
www.OneFlightFiction.com